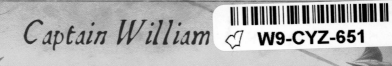

Captain William

Pirateology™
Handbook

A Cabin Boy's Course
in Pirate Hunting

EDITED BY
DUGALD A. STEER AND CLINT TWIST

This book belongs to

....

THE FIVE MILE PRESS
PUBLISHERS OF RARE AND UNUSUAL BOOKS.

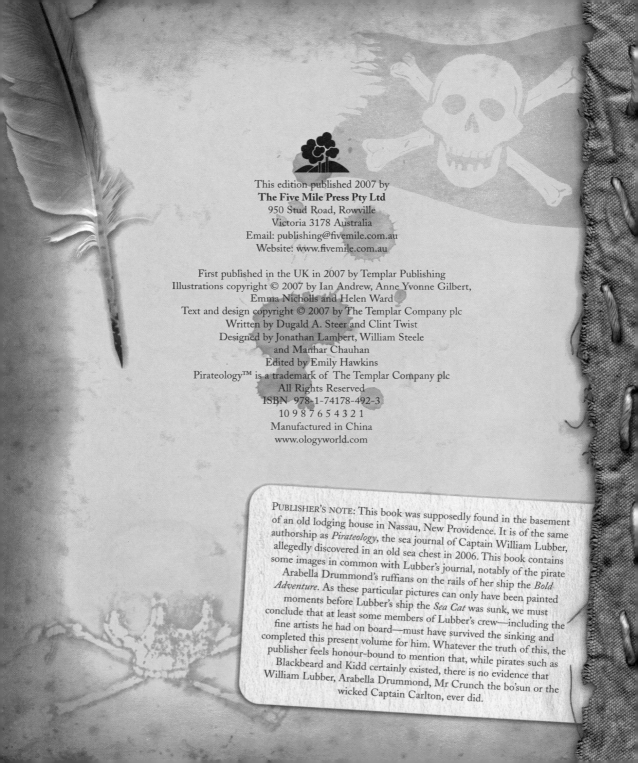

This edition published 2007 by
The Five Mile Press Pty Ltd
950 Stud Road, Rowville
Victoria 3178 Australia
Email: publishing@fivemile.com.au
Website: www.fivemile.com.au

First published in the UK in 2007 by Templar Publishing
Illustrations copyright © 2007 by Ian Andrew, Anne Yvonne Gilbert,
Emma Nicholls and Helen Ward
Text and design copyright © 2007 by The Templar Company plc
Written by Dugald A. Steer and Clint Twist
Designed by Jonathan Lambert, William Steele
and Manhar Chauhan
Edited by Emily Hawkins
Pirateology™ is a trademark of The Templar Company plc
All Rights Reserved
ISBN 978-1-74178-492-3
10 9 8 7 6 5 4 3 2 1
Manufactured in China
www.ologyworld.com

PUBLISHER'S NOTE: This book was supposedly found in the basement of an old lodging house in Nassau, New Providence. It is of the same authorship as *Pirateology*, the sea journal of Captain William Lubber, allegedly discovered in an old sea chest in 2006. This book contains some images in common with Lubber's journal, notably of the pirate Arabella Drummond's ruffians on the rails of her ship the *Bold Adventure*. As these particular pictures can only have been painted moments before Lubber's ship the *Sea Cat* was sunk, we must conclude that at least some members of Lubber's crew—including the fine artists he had on board—must have survived the sinking and completed this present volume for him. Whatever the truth of this, the publisher feels honour-bound to mention that, while pirates such as Blackbeard and Kidd certainly existed, there is no evidence that William Lubber, Arabella Drummond, Mr Crunch the bo'sun or the wicked Captain Carlton, ever did.

By the Command of His Majesty
George, King of England and Scotland,

to Captain William Lubber, Cape Corrientes, Mexico

As you have, during the past twelvemonth, proved your loyalty, competence and personal bravery as our Captain aboard the **Sea Cat**, and have furthermore shown yourself to be an Indefatigable Enemy of Seafaring Rogues and a most successful Pirate Hunter, it is now the **Royal Wish** that you train a number of Young Persons in like manner and encourage in them the same high regard for **Lawful Justice** and **Disdain for Pirates** that you and your crew have so ably demonstrated. You are hereby informed that, should any Young Person show Exceptional Promise as a Pirate Hunter, you have **Licence**, at your sole Discretion and with Suitable Circumstances permitting, to promote them as you see fit, up to and including the rank of **Captain**.

Given under signature and seal on this
4th day of July 1724,

Samuel Shute

Governor-in-Chief over His Majesty's
Territories in Massachusetts

```
IF    _O_
_EEK  _RE___RE
IN _HI_ PL_CE
_O_ _RE ON
_ _ILD
GOO_E
CH__E
```

A=B	G=H	M=N
B=C	H=I	N=O
C=D	I=J	O=P
D=E	J=K	P=Q
E=F	K=L	Q=R
F=G	L=M	R=

```
HE XNT RDDJ SQDZRTQD
HM SGHR OKZBD
XNT ZQD NM Z VHKC
FNNRD BGZRD
```

* Could this curious map and coded message reveal the location of Captain Kidd's missing treasure?

* There's no sight to excite the soul so much as that of your piratical prey at anchor beneath a hunter's moon.

Contents

An Invitation to Brave Souls who would Hunt Down Pirates & Other Seafaring Rogues

If you would dare to join those brave souls who daily risk their lives to make the seas a safer place, then this book, written for the cabin boys aboard the SEA CAT, will be a faithful guide.

Pirate hunting is a most exciting and rewarding profession. I myself am currently engaged in the deadly pursuit of one particularly vicious and intemperate pirate known as Arabella Drummond. I am penning this guide as I sail the seas on her trail.

If you become captain of a pirate-hunting ship, you may count amongst

your expectations a modicum of wealth, obedience from your crew, fear from your enemies and the admiring gratitude of all law-abiding seafarers. You cannot expect to become a captain straightaway, however. To begin with, you must serve an apprenticeship aboard my ship, starting out as a cabin boy. However, if you learn your lessons well—and complete all of the activities set down for your off-watch hours—you may soon progress to the position of able seaman, perhaps then to bo'sun, and eventually to the rank of captain with a ship of your own.

* The amiable bo'sun, Mr Crunch, will be your guide aboard the SEA CAT.

The SEA CAT has been furnished to a suitably warlike degree, with a crew of some 80 brave and experienced seamen. Every one of them is sworn to do his utmost to rid the seas of the piratical menace. As a member of my crew, I expect you to do the same.

The pirate hunter's life is one of action and excitement, but also of great danger. Take heed, therefore, of the lessons in this book, for they may very well save your life one day, or that of one of your shipmates. But be of good cheer—join my crew and together we will destroy the scourge of piracy one and for all!

Captain William Lubber

The Sea Cat, on this, the 21st day of August, 1724

CABIN BOYS REQUIRED
for a Pirate-Hunting Vessel.

OPPORTUNITY FOR
ADVENTURE AND ADVANCEMENT

No previous seafaring experience required as training will be given.
A basic knowledge of reading and writing is essential.

All rations will be provided, plus

A Guaranteed Share of Any Loot
or Treasure that is Recovered.

Apply in person to
Capt. W. Lubber aboard the SEA CAT.

Roster of Cabin Boy's Duties

* Swab the decks
* Serve at the captain's table
* Wash the captain's and bo'sun's clothes
* Load the captain's pistols
* Sharpen the captain's cutlass
* Act as a powder monkey when cannon are used
* Look after any animals, such as the ship's cats and parrots
* Learn the basic pirate flags
* Learn the various parts of the ship
* Learn the essential knots

Ship's Bells

On board, a day is divided into four-hour periods, known as watches. A bell is rung every half hour to mark the passage of time. You will soon learn that 'Second watch, four bells' means six o'clock in the morning—which is when you cabin boys start work.

* Every member of our crew—even lowly cabin boys—must be able to recognise and name these pirate flags.

* Arabella Drummond, the Terror of the Seas

* Blackbeard

* Stede Bonnet

* Edward Low

* Henry Every

* Bartholomew Roberts

* Edward England

The Rank of
CABIN BOY

I bid you welcome aboard the good ship SEA CAT. You are indeed fortunate to have joined our brave company of pirate hunters, and you will be well advised to take careful note of all I say. You will work hard, and for little pay. You will see many strange sights as we scour the oceans for our piratical foes. You will face the same dangers and perils as the rest of the crew — battles, storms, shipwrecks, deadly tropical diseases and a taste of the lash if you misbehave. If your work is satisfactory and a suitable vacancy becomes available through mishap or illness, then in time you may progress to the rank of able seaman — with a corresponding share of the ship's captured goods.

Throughout this handbook there are several amusing activities set down for you to complete in your off-watch hours. The mastery of said activities will help you perform your duties effectively. Now, step lively, pour me a tot of rum and introduce yourself to the kindly Mr Crunch. Mind you are properly respectful when you ask him to show you where the pails and scrubbing brushes are kept.

Captain W. Lubber

Lesson 1:
The Local Menace—
Caribbean Pirates

The most important lesson of all—know your enemy! If you cannot recognise him instantly and understand his every move, then you have very little chance of catching him. Let these pages be your guide to the scurvy rogues you are likely to encounter. First, to our local seafaring scum— those very pirates that infest the tropical blue waters of the Caribbean like the fleas on a fat dog. Although they are not especially brave in combat, they are most notorious for their loud and boastful behaviour.

Caribbean Ports

There have been pirates operating in Caribbean waters for more than 200 years. Port Royal in Jamaica was once the centre of their wicked trade, until a goodly earthquake destroyed a large part of that city in the year of our Lord 1692. Nowadays, you may catch sight of piratical rascals in many a Caribbean port. Take note of their flamboyant clothing and watch how they walk with an unmistakable swagger, not bothering to conceal the weapons they carry at all times.

* Many of these rascals take the utmost pride in their dandified appearance.

* This sea is like a great magnet that attracts pirates from all directions.
Many merchant ships sail between the islands, but the greatest prize is a Spanish
treasure fleet laden with gold and silver from the mines of South America.

Notorious Cruelties

Caribbean pirates have a reputation for greed and cruelty. They often torture their
prisoners, either to make them reveal the whereabouts of hidden gold, or sometimes merely
for sport. Among the worst of this scum was the infamous Blackbeard. He was killed after
a fierce fight by a valiant pirate hunter named Maynard, just a few years ago, in 1718.

* Villainous rogues force a prisoner to dance a jig.

* Blackbeard and Maynard

OFF-WATCH ACTIVITY Copy the map above and
learn the names of the main islands — you are no use as a pirate hunter
if you cannot tell the difference between Cuba, Hispaniola and Jamaica.

Lesson 2:
A Pirate Crew

Although law-abiding seafarers are the steadfast enemies of piratical rogues, there are some similarities between them, as all are sailors. A pirate captain largely has the same requirements for a crew as a pirate hunter like myself. However, whilst all of the SEA CAT's crew are volunteers, not all members of a pirate crew are aboard by choice.

The Captain

It will come as no surprise that the most important member of a pirate crew is the captain. And just because he (or very rarely she) is a pirate, it does not mean that he is absolutely lacking intelligence—it is no easy thing to be the captain of any kind of a ship, and pirate captains are often very wily indeed. Second in command will be a bo'sun or a sailing master.

The Crew

A pirate ship has need of the same special skills as any other ship. It needs a sailmaker to sew the canvas sails, a carpenter to make repairs to damaged timbers and a good cook to keep the rest of the crew fit and well.

* A ship's gunner and sailmaker.

A Note on Pay Aboard the SEA CAT

Any vessels captured or goods recovered shall be valued at the Custom's House when we reach port in terms of the silver coins known commonly as dollars. The agreed sum shall be divided into 200 shares to be distributed as follows: 100 shares to the investors in Boston, Massachusetts, 15 shares to the captain, 5 shares to the bo'sun and 1 share to each of the 80 able seamen. Thus for every $800 recovered the investors receive $400, each seaman shall receive $4, the bo'sun $20 and the captain $60. As a cabin boy you have no entitlement to anything except food and board—but if we strike it very rich, I have no doubt that your generous shipmates will throw you a small coin or two.

Clockwise from bottom left: unlucky surgeon, able seaman, gunner, serving maid, captain, bo'sun

Ships' Surgeons

* A pirate crew kidnap a surgeon.

The crews of merchant ships expect peaceful voyages so they are equipped only to deal with minor accidents. Pirates, however, expect to receive wounds in armed combat, so they often try to ensure they have an experienced surgeon on board, even if he is an unwilling guest who has been kidnapped.

OFF-WATCH ACTIVITY Now it won't hurt you to stretch your brains with some mathematical figuring of a monetary nature. If we return to port with goods valued at $20,000, how much will the captain receive? What would each able seaman take home?

Lesson 3:
The Parts of a Ship

Do not start feeling too pleased with yourself until you have learned the name of every part of a ship. It is absolutely vital that you can tell fore from aft and port from starboard. This is not mere book learning for book learning's sake — in stormy conditions, when the sails are being torn to shreds overhead, knowing the difference could well be a matter of life or death.

All sailing ships, whether merchant, naval or pirate, are built in the same way and have the same general features. Pirates often remove some of the upper decks fore and aft to give themselves a flat, open space for fighting. They also strip away the safety rails and add as many extra cannon as they can get their thieving hands upon.

* The crow's nest is a lookout platform set near the top of a mast.

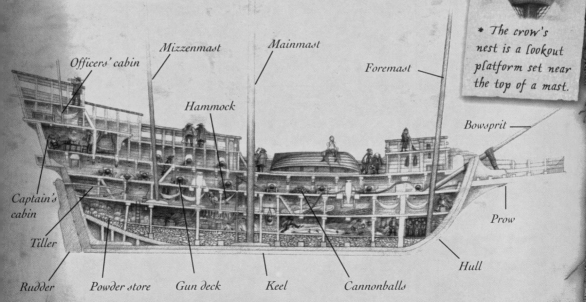

Officers' cabin

Mizzenmast

Mainmast

Foremast

Hammock

Bowsprit

Captain's cabin

Prow

Tiller

Rudder

Powder store

Gun deck

Keel

Cannonballs

Hull

Compass directions are used when plotting the ship's course, but the crew use a different set of directions when passing on instructions. Commit this to memory: 'fore' means towards the front (bow) of the ship, while 'aft' means towards the back (stern). When facing the bow, 'port' is to your left-hand side and 'starboard' is to your right.

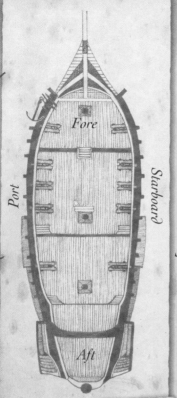

The canvas sails are hoisted from long timbers known as yards that are attached across the masts at right angles. This ship is steered by means of a lever called a tiller that moves the rudder from side to side. Most modern ships have a ship's wheel instead of a tiller.

Mainmast

Yards

Foremast

Mizzenmast

Stern

Bow

The capstan is a type of winch or windlass that is used to raise the anchor.

The ship's bell is rung to mark each half hour of a four-hour watch.

A heavy iron anchor keeps the ship moored to the sea bed.

OFF-WATCH ACTIVITY Test your knowledge of directions aboard a ship—and no cheating! If you face aft, which is the port side—left or right? If you face starboard, which way to the bow? If you are standing on deck, in which direction is the keel?

15

Lesson 4:
Handy Knots & Hitches

Mind you make an early acquaintance with rope—it is both a blessing and a curse for sailors. It is a blessing because the masts and sails are held in place by yards and yards of rope, called rigging; and a curse because there is never to be found a piece of rope of exactly the right length. For this reason, everyone on board—even lowly cabin boys—must know their knots. There's no place on this ship for a dunderhead who cannot tell a reef knot from a bowline.

* Tying a reef knot

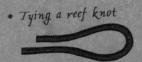  

A reef knot fastens two ends of rope of the same thickness, and is sometimes called a square knot. A loop is formed at one end, and another loop made around and through the first and pulled tight. We use this knot to tie the sails close to the yards when they are 'reefed' (furled) because the wind is too strong.

* Making a bowline knot

A bowline knot makes a secure loop at one end of a piece of rope. It is often used when tying up a small boat at a quayside, with a single rope attached to the bow—this is how the knot gets its name.

There are many other ways of tying rope that all cabin boys must learn. Generally, although not always, knots that join two ropes are called 'bends' while knots that join a rope to an object are called 'hitches'.

* A clove hitch is used to tie a rope to a rail.

* A sheepshank shortens a piece of rope without the need for cutting.

* A sailor's knot is used for tying together thick ropes.

* A figure-of-eight knot is used to make a stop-knot in a length of rope.

* A sheet bend joins two ropes of slightly different thickness.

* Threading a rope around a set of rollers, which are called a 'block and tackle', makes it possible to lift heavy objects, such as boxes crammed with gold coins, without too much difficulty, as shown here.

OFF-WATCH ACTIVITY Practise tying these knots until you can make them with your eyes closed — then try tying them with pieces of wet cord, like a true sailor.

Lesson 5:
The Jolly Boat & Sloop

"Swing the lead!" "Jump to the jolly boat and follow that sloop!"
You must know the meaning of these orders if you wish to progress. Pirates favour vessels with a shallow draft, such as the sloop, which allow them to enter bays not deep enough for larger ships. To pursue them, the savvy pirate hunter must know how to make good use of the effective little jolly boat.

SLOOP

The Sloop

Pirates have learned all the advantages of the sloop. In addition to its shallow draft, this small ship normally has a very long bowsprit, which enables extra sail to be carried, adding both speed and manoeuvrability. A well built sloop is able to reach speeds of more than 10 knots with a good wind.

* Sailors measure the water's depth with a length of cord attached to a weight called a lead. The cord is marked at intervals of one fathom (about 6 1/2 feet). When the lead is dropped to the sea bed, the depth of water can be read.

Hiding from Justice

A single-masted sloop, such as the one shown here, can carry a crew of up to 50 and makes an ideal vessel for pirates who operate in coastal waters. It may be armed with ten or more guns and its crew is sufficient in number to make successful attacks on all but the very largest targets. It can also easily evade attack from large warships patrolling in the area by sailing into rivers and lagoons.

The Jolly Boat

The jolly boat, which is an open rowing boat, is a useful piece of equipment. As well as chasing pirates through the shallows, it may be used to ferry passengers and cargo to and from the shore, or to make an attack on a pirate ship at anchor.

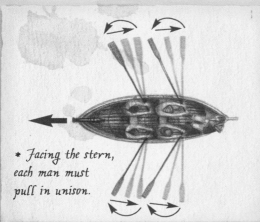

* Facing the stern, each man must pull in unison.

The Art of Rowing

Rowing a jolly boat is a matter of teamwork that requires constant practice. Each man must perform the same actions — sweeping back the oar-blade, dropping it into the water and pulling hard on the oar before lifting it clear of the surface — at exactly the same time, and over and over again — in order for the boat to make smooth and steady progress.

OFF-WATCH ACTIVITY A knotted cord is a very useful measuring instrument. Make your own by taking a cord and tying a figure-of-eight knot at 12-inch or 1-inch intervals, depending on the length of your cord. Then practise taking measurements.

Lesson 6:
Food & Drink on Board

A well-fed pirate is a happy pirate—and the same is true for all honest sailors. As cabin boys, you will serve me at my table with the best available food and drink. Be warned, however, that I have a hearty appetite and I leave few scraps—you and the rest of the lower-ranking crew will often have to make do with ship's biscuits and a swig of water.

* Rule number one—do not blame the cook. He can only prepare what we carry, and there is not much that even the best cook can do to make salted fish, salted meat and ship's biscuit any the more appetising.

* The Cook

Fine Dining

The great virtue of salted food and biscuits is that they keep well. They may not be very tasty, but they remain edible after weeks, even months, in the ship's stores. Fresh food is a rare treat. The best parts of any fish that are caught go to the captain's table. Sea turtles are easy prey and can be kept alive in a tank of water until they are needed for the pot. The juice of limes, which is exceedingly sour, is believed to prevent the sickness known as scurvy that afflicts sailors who eat little fresh food.

*Whatever your tipple, whether it be water, wine or rum, you will most likely drink it from a blackjack—a leather drinking cup that will not break like clay cups or glass if it receives a knock.

The Smokehouse

Smoking meat and fish helps preserve it, and some would say gives a better flavour than salting. The problem with smoking is that it requires a special smokehouse to be built and a great deal of fire wood to be collected.

A Pirate Jig

A good meal—perhaps roasted wildfowl or fresh fish—is reason enough for any sailor to celebrate, and pirates are no exception. If there are no pirate hunters around, they will sing and dance after a hearty dinner until they fall down from exhaustion or, more likely, an excess of rum.

OFF-WATCH ACTIVITY To make ship's biscuits, add a pinch of salt to 450g of wholemeal flour, and enough water to make a stiff dough. Leave for half an hour, then roll out and separate into biscuits. Put them on a baking tray, then ask the cook to place them in a hot oven for half an hour. Put the biscuits on a rack and leave them to cool.

Lesson 7:
The Cautionary Tale of Edward England

The moral of this tale is that pirates are evil-hearted rogues who will not hesitate to turn against one of their own kind—even if it is their captain—should he but make the mistake of behaving like a civilised and gentlemanly fellow.

Edward England was that rare creature—a pirate with a streak of decency and mercy, and this was to prove his downfall. He began his piratical career under the command of a certain Captain Winter who sailed out of New Providence in the Bahamas. The arrival in 1717 of a Governor of the Bahamas of strongly anti-piratical mind made life very difficult for England and his companions, so he decided to take a ship and try his luck on the other side of the Atlantic Ocean.

Initially, it proved to be a wise decision. There were rich pickings to be had in the waters off the western coast of Africa, and he sank or seized many ships. Captain England was so successful that he renamed his ship the VICTORY, but soon afterwards his luck ran out due to a simple act of friendliness towards other pirates.

In the year 1719, the VICTORY encountered another pirate vessel, the CASSANDRA, which was crammed with gold and silver as its crew had enjoyed even greater success. Instead of seizing the other vessel, Captain England merely toasted their mutual success with rum and let the CASSANDRA continue without hindrance.

The crew of the VICTORY took a pretty dim view of their captain's decision to allow the CASSANDRA to go free so they marooned him on the island of Mauritius, along with three seamen that they did not trust. The VICTORY, now commanded by a new captain, sailed off in pursuit of the CASSANDRA.

* Edward England chose a simple skull-and-crossbones as his flag. Despite his dismal fate, his flag has become the most famous of all the Jolly Rogers.

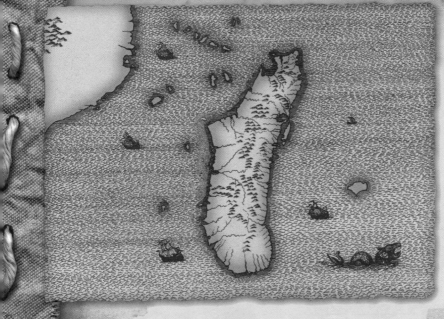

Now, as you should well know, Mauritius is no desert island. The former Captain England and his companions might well have prospered had they been better equipped, because wild food is to be found in abundance—especially a most tasty bird called the dodo that is exceedingly easy to catch. However, lacking both tools and weapons, there was little the marooned victims could do to exploit their surroundings.

Using their bare hands, they fabricated a crude but seaworthy craft from pieces of driftwood tied together, and managed to sail to the much larger island of Madagascar. Once there, they were able to beg charity from some of the pirates who had made homes for themselves around the coast of that island.

I have no further information about the other three, but to the best of my knowledge Edward England is still there, a once proud ship's captain now living like a common beggar—a pirate who made the mistake of not being quite piratical enough.

* Beware if you visit Madagascar and a bearded vagabond who claims that he was once a notorious pirate tries to extract money from you.

Roster of Able Seaman's Duties

* Climb up and down the rigging with ease
* Raise and lower the anchor
* Act as lookout
* Recognise national flags
* Man the oars of the jolly boat when necessary
* Operate the wheel or tiller
* Keep weapons in good order
* Act as gunner
* Take part in hand-to-hand fighting
* Go ashore in search of food or water
* Assist in careening the ship

Hours of Work

As you should know by now, each 24-hour day is divided into four-hour shifts called watches. Able seamen usually work alternate watches, and they try and catch some shuteye in between. In bad weather, however, you may have to work non-stop for three or four watches without a break.

* Able seamen must often act as gunners.

It requires skill and practise to operate guns in the heat of battle. A good gunner is one who can perform his duties calmly and correctly while cannon thunder all around him. Able seamen must familiarise themselves with all the procedures relating to cannon and ammunition. If a gunner falls in battle, any seaman may be called upon as a replacement.

The Rank of
ABLE SEAMAN

Congratulations on being promoted to the rank of able seaman. I confess that your rapid progress has been something of a surprise to me considering your wretched state of ignorance when you first came aboard. It is greatly to be hoped that your success will not lead to complacency and idleness — you may be a fully-fledged seaman, but there is a good deal more still to be learned. Your new rank brings new responsibilities, so you must keep your head down and work hard.

Take special note of this — if any man falls asleep while on lookout duty, he will certainly earn a taste of the lash. Now, jump to it! Set about your duties straightaway unless you want to be cleaning out the bilges for the rest of the voyage.

Captain W. Lubber

Lesson 8:
Privateers & Buccaneers

Names do not much matter when cannonballs are flying through the air; but every able seaman should easily be able to tell the difference between privateers, buccaneers and pirates. Privateers are sometimes law-abiding fellows, although their deeds can betray more roguish tendencies, but pirates and buccaneers are always to be hunted down as brigands and criminals.

* Pirate

* Buccaneer

* Privateer

Pirates

A pirate is any man or woman who commits acts of robbery at sea. Piracy is as old as seafaring itself, and has become a traditional occupation in some parts of the world. No matter what they claim to be, pirates are simply criminals who deserve the direst of punishments.

Buccaneers

A buccaneer, sometimes called a freebooter, was an English or French settler in the Caribbean who turned to piracy during the 17th century. The city of Port Royal in Jamaica and the small island of Tortuga were the main bases for these evildoers.

Privateers

A privateer is a seafarer who claims that his actions are justified by a letter of marque. During times of war, governments have been known to issue these letters, which permit the holder to capture or destroy ships belonging to an enemy nation. Many so-called privateers, however, are not fussy about which ships they attack.

Captain William Kidd

* William Kidd

Captain Kidd was a former British naval officer who became a pirate hunter at the age of 40. He sailed under a letter of marque issued by the Governor of New York, which gave him authority to capture any pirates he encountered. However, Kidd soon turned pirate himself, attacking and robbing a merchant ship. Soon after, he was arrested and was hanged in London in 1701.

* l'Ollonais

The Tortuga Freebooters

The French pirate known as l'Ollonais was one of the most ferocious and ruthless of the Tortuga buccaneers. He not only attacked dozens of Spanish ships, but also raided Spanish ports and towns on the American mainland. He was shipwrecked in 1668, after which the rogue was unfortunate enough to be eaten by cannibals.

OFF-WATCH ACTIVITY A soldier named Hernándo Cortés led the Spanish conquest of Mexico and Central America. See what you can find out about his life and achievements.

Lesson 9:
Letters of Marque &
the Pirates' Code

My crew should be assured that the SEA CAT sails under an authentic letter of marque issued by the Governor of Massachusetts. If any man questions our lawful authority, then he may come and read the letter for himself—and woe betide any seaman who has not learned his ABCs well enough to read.

The Laws of the Sea

In peacetime, the actions of a ship's captain are largely governed by the unwritten rules of the sea, which have become entrenched over thousands of years of seafaring, and cover such matters as rights of salvage and the quarantine measures to be taken if there is an outbreak of disease. In wartime, however, the situation is different. Any ship flying the flag of a hostile nation may be considered a legitimate target, even if it is sailing without hostile intent. As far as our voyage is concerned, we are pirate hunters duly authorised by letter of marque, so you may consider any ship that is guilty of piratical behaviour as a target to be captured or destroyed.

To Capt. Daniel Plowman, Commander of the Briganteen Charles of Boston,

Whereas Her Sacred Majesty **Anne** by the Grace of **God** of England, Scotland, France and Ireland, Hath an Open War against France and Spain, their Vassals and Subjects. And Forasmuch as you have made Application unto Me for Licence to Arm, Furnish and Equip the said Briganteen in Warlike manner, against Her Majesty's said Enemies, I do accordingly Permit the same; And, Reposing special Trust in your Loyalty and good Conduct, by Virtue of the Authorities contained in Her Majesty's Royal Commission, Empower you to be Commander of the said Briganteen Charles, Hereby Authorising you to War, Fight, Take, Kill, Suppress and Destroy, any Pirates, Privateers, or other the Subjects and Vassals of France, or Spain, the Declared Enemies of the Crown of England; Their Ships, Vessels and Goods, to take and make Prize of. Given under my Seal at Arms at Boston the Thirteenth Day of July: In the Second Year of Her Majesty's Reign, Annoque Domini, 1703.

Isaac Addington, Secr.

* A letter of marque issued on behalf of Queen Anne to license pirate hunters in the year of our lord 1703.

* Although pirates are naught but a bunch of criminal vermin, and clearly do not venture abroad with letters of marque, most are bound by common sense and regard for their own safety to follow the same basic shipboard rules as honest sailors.

Misdemeanours to Avoid

There will be no fighting, neither with weapons nor bare fists, among the crew — save it for the enemy. If a dispute should arise between crewmates, then it shall be settled by words, not by violent actions. If peaceable conversation fails to resolve the dispute then the captain shall decide the matter, and shall have the final word.

No member of the crew shall desert his post or otherwise attempt to leave the ship's company without proper permission. Any man wishing to depart the ship would be well advised to think again. The penalty for desertion is death or marooning.

There will be no general carousing without the captain's consent. The lights will be put out at 8 o'clock, after which time any man still inclined to drink may walk out on the open deck.

OFF-WATCH ACTIVITY As you know, it is important to try and understand the enemy, and so give yourself a better chance of catching him. Imagine that you are a pirate. Draw up your own list of rules, or articles, for life on board your ship.

Lesson 10:
A Pirate's Possessions

Pirates are by nature an acquisitive bunch of rogues, but they are very choosy about which items they keep for themselves. Some are attracted by glitter and sparkle, and festoon themselves with stolen jewellery and gaudy clothing. Others, who are perhaps more sober-minded than their outlandish colleagues, concentrate on picking out the best quality weapons and equipment.

* Greatcoat

* Fine clothes

* Belt with purse

* Sea boots

Fine and fancy clothes of silk or cotton are easy for a pirate to acquire; more difficult are a decent pair of boots of the right size and a strong leather belt. Salt water and sea air can have a terrible effect on leather unless it is kept well oiled.

Your average pirate is not a trusting person. He keeps his coins in a purse that is fastened to a leather belt around his waist. Any other possessions, such as spare clothes or stolen booty, are stored inside a stout and securely locked sea chest.

* Sea chest

* Booty

* Needle and thread

* Three-cornered hat

* Headscarf

* Silk sash

Some pirates wear a headscarf to cover their greasy, matted hair, and others prefer to shave themselves completely bald to prevent lice. The most audacious rogues proudly sport three-cornered hats upon their heads, just like the ones worn by naval officers. A brightly coloured silk sash is not just for show — it is also a handy place to wedge a pair of pistols.

OFF-WATCH ACTIVITY Pirates must be able to make and mend. You will need to learn how to mend torn clothes or add patches to knees and elbows to make them more hard-wearing. There is a certain skill in sewing without pricking your fingers with the needle — find someone who can teach you to sew a simple patch onto another piece of cloth.

Lesson 11:
Seizing Ships

Despite a few tales of pirates actually buying their ships, these rascals rarely come into possession of a vessel through lawful means. There are several proven cases of a ship owner deciding to turn pirate, then persuading his crew to join him in his criminal voyaging. More often, however, the vessel is stolen. In recent times pirates have employed various stratagems, including deception and incitement to mutiny, to achieve their wicked intentions.

Deception!

Pirates are not over-endowed with intelligence, but neither are they without a certain low cunning. It has been known for a group of them to gain admittance to a ship under pretext of joining the crew.

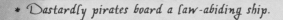

* Dastardly pirates board a law-abiding ship.

Then, once the unlucky vessel is at sea, its new piratical crew members will overpower the captain and seize control of the ship. If their numbers are insufficient for this task, they will assist their dastardly companions in climbing aboard.

Mutiny!

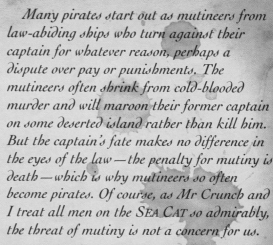

Many pirates start out as mutineers from law-abiding ships who turn against their captain for whatever reason, perhaps a dispute over pay or punishments. The mutineers often shrink from cold-blooded murder and will maroon their former captain on some deserted island rather than kill him. But the captain's fate makes no difference in the eyes of the law — the penalty for mutiny is death — which is why mutineers so often become pirates. Of course, as Mr Crunch and I treat all men on the SEA CAT so admirably, the threat of mutiny is not a concern for us.

Another favoured stratagem is to steal a ship from harbour while most of the crew are ashore carousing. Under cover of darkness, some of the pirates climb aboard and silence the lookouts, while others cut the mooring ropes.

Pirates will usually give a ship the chance to surrender, but once they hoist the red flag (which means 'no quarter') the crew aboard the hapless vessel can expect no mercy but a swift death.

OFF-WATCH ACTIVITY Draw a plan of a ship and mark the positions where you would place your lookouts if you were captain. Then, work out a plan pirates might use in order to approach the ship unseen.

Lesson 12:
The Merchant & Brigantine

It is imperative that all able seamen become thoroughly acquainted with the workings of our good vessel the SEA CAT. Our ship is a type of Dutch merchant ship that has been converted to hunt pirates by increasing its number of guns. Unfortunately some pirates think along similar lines, converting captured merchant ships for piratical ends by modifying them in the same fashion. The brigantine, smaller and shapelier than the merchant ship, is another type of pirate ship that you ought to familiarise yourself with.

QUEEN ANNE'S REVENGE

A three-masted merchant ship measures about 100 feet, with cargo packed into holds beneath the gun deck. Most merchant vessels carry between 10 and 20 cannon to defend themselves. One of the most feared pirate vessels of all was Blackbeard's the QUEEN ANNE'S REVENGE. He converted her from a humble merchant ship to the most powerful ship in American waters by loading her with 40 cannon.

BRIGANTINE

A brigantine is up to 80 feet long and has only two masts. The sails are most ingeniously arranged with the masts carrying square sails, but also supporting the triangular sails that give the brigantine extra speed through the water, especially when the wind is blowing hard.

The captain and bo'sun use a pair of dividers to measure the ship's progress on a map. The distance between the two points of the dividers can be adjusted to represent the distance the ship has sailed in one day.

To measure speed, a seaman lowers the end of a long knotted rope over the side and allows it to trail behind the ship. By counting the number of knots that go over the side in a given time, he can estimate how fast the ship is travelling.

OFF-WATCH ACTIVITY Find a map that has a scale showing distances in miles. If you do not have any dividers, mark the scale on a piece of card. Then, use this card to measure how far it is between various points on the map.

Lesson 13:
Identifying Ships at Sea

It is no good you acting as lookout up there in the crow's nest if you cannot tell the captain what you see, so you must pay special attention to learning your flags. All law-abiding ships are proud to bear their nation's flag, and some pirates have the same attitude about the filthy rags that flutter from their masts. Be wary, as pirates often keep a stock of different flags on board purposefully to pretend that they are on an innocent mission.

| VENICE Red Flag | MALTA | GENOA | GREAT BRITAIN Red Ensign | GREAT BRITAIN Union Flag | SCOTLAND Saltire |

| CORSICA | FRANCE Royal Standard | FRANCE Naval Ensign | DENMARK | BRITISH EAST INDIA COMPANY | NEW ENGLAND |

| HOLLAND | DUTCH EAST INDIA COMPANY | DUTCH WEST INDIA COMPANY | SWEDEN | PRUSSIA Brandenburg | POLAND |

| SPAIN Royal Standard | CASTILE & LEON | PORTUGAL | PORTUGAL Knights of Christ | HAMBURG Hanseatic League | MUSCOVY |

| OTTOMAN EMPIRE | SICILY. | SARDINIA | ALGERIA Barbary Ensign | TUNISIA Privateers' Flag | CHINA Dragon Flag |

These are the flags you are likely to see in this the year of our Lord 1724, flying from the mastheads of merchant or naval ships or fluttering above official buildings. Every able seaman should note that flags are always changing, so you must be alert to developments.

Pirate Flags

　　You have already learned these pirate flags—all of which bear some part of the human skeleton—but there are almost as many different flags as there are pirates. On one of his flags, Bart Roberts chose to portray himself brandishing a sword while standing on two skulls to represent Barbados and Martinique. The Indian Ocean pirate Thomas Tew bore on his flag a single arm brandishing a curved scimitar. Many other pirates make use of an hourglass, symbolising that their victims' time is all but run out.

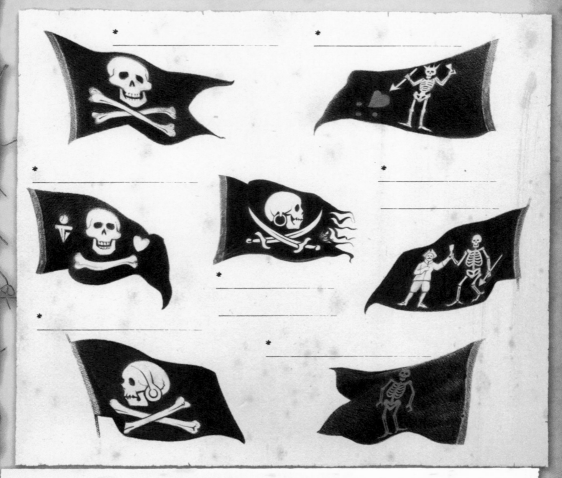

OFF-WATCH ACTIVITY *You should now be able to recognise all of these pirate flags, which you learned when you were a cabin boy (page 8). Can you remember who they belong to? Fill in these names next to the appropriate flags: Arabella Drummond, Blackbeard, Edward Low, Edward England, Stede Bonnet, Henry Every, Bartholomew Roberts. Now design your own flag using any of the following symbols: skeleton, sword, hourglass, heart, spear, dagger, drinking cup. Use only black, white, yellow and red.*

Lesson 14:
The Cautionary Tale of Major Stede Bonnet

Mind you take heed of this story of roguery born of idleness and an unwise marriage—how one William Bonnet chose to live a pirate's life and so suffered a pirate's death, dangling at the end of a rope. Some law-abiding people take it into their heads to go pirating as though it were some sort of adventure. It is not, and Bonnet certainly paid the price for his foolishness.

Mr William Bonnet enjoyed an entirely comfortable life as a bachelor in Barbados, where his family owned a large plantation, but his woes began almost as soon as he married. The new Mrs Bonnet seems to have been a most disagreeable woman who complained constantly, and Mr Bonnet soon tired of this marital strife and went away to sea.

Being a wealthy man with a deep-seated sense of mischief, he purchased a ship with ten cannon, renamed it the REVENGE and set about becoming a pirate. Styling himself 'Major Stede Bonnet', he attacked and plundered several ships sailing from ports in Virginia and Carolina. His success might have continued indefinitely if he had not had the great misfortune to encounter that notorious pirate Blackbeard.

The two met peaceably enough, but Bonnet was outclassed and outwitted. His crew sided with Blackbeard and the REVENGE was taken from him. Infuriated by this turn of events Bonnet swore to kill Blackbeard but, alas, he never got the opportunity, as he never saw him again.

Bonnet no longer found piracy sufficiently diverting, so he decided to hang-up his headscarf, surrender to the King's Pardon and retire to dry land. Although he appeared to settle down quietly enough, he never quite became a respectable citizen. His face was marked with a vivid scar, a souvenir of some desperate shipboard encounter. Many ladies found this disfigurement to be attractive, while their husbands enjoyed such excitements as might be found in the company of an ex-pirate.

But life on land soon proved even more tiresome than Bonnet remembered, and he was unable to resist the lure of the sea. He acquired another ship—a rather leaky sloop that he named the ROYAL JAMES, and adopted the alias 'Captain Thomas' so as to conceal his identity. He took up his

* Through force of personality Blackbeard was able to take control of Bonnet's ship.

piratical career where he had left off, raiding the same shipping routes as before. Although he managed to steal little of any real value, his activities soon became a nuisance to the authorities in Carolina and they sent two ships to hunt him down.

Early one morning in September 1718, near the mouth of Cape Fear River, the hunters sighted their prey and battle commenced. The pirates fought viciously, killing 12 sailors and wounding twice as many again, but they could not withstand the combined

gunfire of the valiant pirate hunters and were at last defeated. 'Captain Thomas' was captured and his true identity discovered. The authorities were less than pleased to find that the rogue Bonnet had already been pardoned once, but had returned to piracy.

Bonnet was put under house arrest at Charles Town in Carolina, but he shortly escaped along with one of his companions. Although the escapees managed to find a small boat, they were soon intercepted and the companion was shot dead. Bonnet was recaptured and put on trial in November 1718. He was found guilty of piracy, and was sentenced to death and duly hanged.

Roster of Bo'sun's Duties

* Manage the sails, rigging and ship's course
* Supervise the crew
* Take charge of the ship's stores
* Learn to use the compass, backstaff and other navigational equipment
* Become familiar with the ports most often used by pirates
* Take control of the ship if the captain is killed or absent
* Command the guns during engagements
* Dole out punishments, including the lash, when necessary

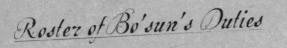

* A good bo'sun must be as familiar with a compass rose as he is with the back of his hands.

* The bo'sun is entitled to hang his hammock in the officers' cabin, which is quieter than the crew's quarters — although the surgeon who shares the cabin has a reputation for loud snoring.

The Rank of
BO'SUN

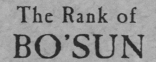

Hearty congratulations on your promotion to bo'sun, sir, after the untimely death of the late incumbent. You have learned your lessons well, displaying great courage indeed in recovering poor Mr Crunch's body from the grips of those ungodly cannibals before they might eat him. We'll get under way presently, as soon as we have given that poor soul a decent burial at sea.

Be sure to carry out your new duties with due care and attention—it is a heavy responsibility for one so young, and you must work hard to earn the respect of the rest of the crew who were so recently your equals. Now, make those lads dance to your tune and be quick about it! Show them what it means to be a real pirate hunter!

Captain W. Lubber

Lesson 15:
Barbary Corsairs

Make no mistake: 'corsair' is just another word for pirate, and all who sail the Mediterranean Sea live in constant fear of these blackhearted villains. 'Barbary' is the name given to that portion of North Africa stretching from the Pillars of Hercules to the Gulf of Sirte, which has been infested with seafaring thieves for several hundred years. The corsairs enjoy some degree of protection from the Ottoman Sultan, who is the overlord of North Africa.

On Board a Corsair Galley

You will find two types of person aboard a corsair ship, apart from any recent prisoners they have captured. There are the corsairs themselves, who generally dress according to the style of the North African Muslim lands, and there are the slaves that man the oars, who will be wearing rags if they are dressed at all. The Mediterranean Sea has very changeable winds, so most of its ships are galleys, with oars as well as sails, so that they can proceed by rowing when there is no suitable wind.

     * Muslim scimitar

     * Italian rapier

* Although they do not lack firearms, many corsairs prefer to fight with a sword — either a curved Muslim scimitar or a captured Italian rapier.

A Barbary Battering

The corsair galley is a narrow craft that is little altered from an ancient Roman galley. Because they were invented before the age of gunpowder, Mediterranean galleys are not designed to make the best use of cannon. Their chief means of attack is the ram that extends from the bow. Propelled by its oars, a galley can manoeuvre itself to punch its ram through the timbers of an opposing vessel.

* Though mainly confined to the Mediterranean Sea, the Barbary corsairs do not fear to venture into the Atlantic Ocean. Last century, in the year 1631, they had the audacity to raid the village of Baltimore in Ireland to carry off slaves and booty.

* The main Barbary ports—Algiers, Salé, Tangiers, Tripoli and Tunis— are veritable pirate fortresses, so the brave pirate hunter can have no expectation of friendship or assistance from any of their inhabitants.

Corsica

Sardinia

Pillars of Hercules

Sicily

Tangiers

Tunis

Salé

Algiers

MEDITERRANEAN SEA

Gulf of Sirte

Tripoli

OFF-WATCH ACTIVITY A bo'sun must know the waters he travels in. Study the map above for one minute, then cover it and see if you can remember all the ports and the shape of the coastline. Try to redraw the map from memory.

Lesson 16:
The Barbarossa Brothers

Most feared of all the Barbary corsairs were the two brothers who were known by the same name—Barbarossa, which means 'Redbeard'.

The elder brother was born in the middle of the 15th century on the Greek island of Lesbos. He was an ambitious young man and he converted to Islam, taking the name Aruj, in order to join a Turkish pirate crew. Aruj proved to be a very quick learner and his progress through the pirate ranks was remarkably rapid. As a captain, he made a dramatic debut when he used trickery to capture two galleys belonging to the Pope. Easily recognisable by his red beard, he soon became leader of a small fleet of pirate ships that were feared throughout the whole of the Mediterranean. No ships, not even those protected by the mighty Knights of Malta, were safe from Barbarossa's savage attacks.

By the beginning of the 16th century, Barbarossa's power and ambition had outstripped the ability of his Turkish masters to control him. He broke away from the Turks and invaded Algeria. From this base he extended his power into neighbouring Morocco and Tunisia, and threatened to put the whole of the North African coast under his rule. Alarmed by his power, some of the local Algerian chieftains sent an envoy to Charles V, King of Spain and Holy Roman Emperor.

Alerted to the threat posed by Barbarossa, Charles V ordered 10,000 of Europe's finest soldiers to sail to Algiers and dethrone this upstart pirate. Although Aruj and his band of cutthroats resisted stoutly, they were no match for Charles's battle-hardened troops, so the first Barbarossa was killed at Tlemcen in 1518.

The younger brother, named Khair-ed-Din, who also had a red beard, survived the fighting. After the European troops had returned home the wily villain somehow managed to regain control of Algeria. Realising that he could not defend himself against foreign armies, he made formal submission to the Turkish sultan. In return for acknowledging the sultan as his overlord, Khair-ed-Din received the protection of 2,000 janissaries—the Turkish troops that were feared and respected by all that encountered them. Encouraged by his new allies, the second Barbarossa continued the piratical onslaught begun by his brother.

* Armed with a curved scimitar and a pistol, Khair-ed-Din prepares to leap aboard a Spanish galleon.

Merchant ships sailed in constant terror of attack as the pirates defeated all warships that were sent against them. Khair-ed-Din grew immensely rich and lived to the ripe old age of 80. After his death in 1546, rumours began to circulate in Europe that it had been impossible to bury his body because his soul was so evil that even the devil himself rejected it.

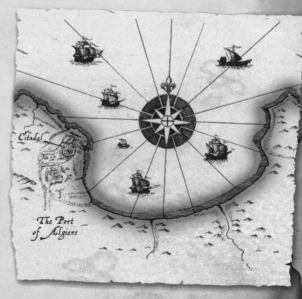

Citadel

The Port of Algiers

* Khair-ed-Din made the port of Algiers his base. Situated on a bay sheltered from storms, Algiers has been a pirate stronghold for hundreds of years. The towering ramparts of the citadel dominate the harbour. Cannon mounted on the walls will soon sink any pirate hunter who dares approach this filthy nest of vipers.

45

Lesson 17:
Navigational Equipment &
Sea Charts

If the captain, through some malady, mischance or misdeed, becomes unfit or unable to command the ship, then you are next in line. Therefore it is of prime importance for your own survival, as well as that of your shipmates, that you know how to find your way around the trackless expanses of the open sea. If you have not already done so, now is the time to learn the use of navigational equipment.

* Backstaff

* Compass

* Spyglass,
or telescope

* Dividers

Skills of the Navigator

The key to good navigation is to know the ship's location in relation to a sea chart. Your position north or south of the equator can be calculated by using a backstaff to measure the angle to the sun when it is highest in the sky.

The ship's east-west position cannot be determined by astronomical observations, so you must rely on your compass readings and a good estimate of the ship's speed.

* Prevailing winds around the world

Northeast Trades

Southeast Trades

SE & SW Monsoons

NE & SW Monsoons

Prevailing Westwardly Winds

Calms of Cancer

Equatorial Calms

Calms of Capricorn

* A waggoner is a chart made especially for identifying coastal features, named after a Dutch chart maker called Lucas Waghenaer.

Navigational Charts

Good sea charts are the most invaluable aids to navigation. They show the accurate locations of coastlines and islands, and the best also give information on the depth of the sea and warnings about hidden reefs or rocks. Sea charts are also available that show the trade winds that blow around the world and the monsoon winds, which change direction every six months.

It is advisable to develop a skill for drawing so you can make your own charts of notorious piratical haunts. In addition to indicating the shape of bays, islands and underwater obstacles, a good waggoner will also give some indication of the terrain behind the shoreline. Over the years the charts used by ships' pilots have become more accurate. Early waggoners were quite simple, yet latterly, as this chart of the sandbanks around Ocracoke Inlet shows, they have become more detailed.

OFF-WATCH ACTIVITY Try making some charts of your own, taking care to make a note of all key landmarks of the area you are studying.

47

Lesson 18:
Pirate Ports

Often it is the stink that gives pirate ports away—with an offshore wind blowing, you can invariably smell them from many miles off. A pirate captain has few choices if he wants to put into harbour. He and his crew are liable to be arrested on sight at any law-abiding port, so they tend to gather like flies on rotting food at lawless places located near the main sailing routes for merchant ships.

PORT ROYAL IN 1692 EARTHQUAKE

Port Royal in Jamaica became one of the most notorious pirate haunts in the whole world. In 1692 an earthquake caused a large part of the city to be shaken apart and engulfed by the sea, thus washing away a great deal of piratical filth. Within ten years, the law-abiding survivors had commenced the rebuilding of Port Royal under the direction of the island's governor.

The Pirate Chieftain

There are few parts of the world that do not have a local pirate's den. In some places, pirates have established control over a sufficiently large area for it to be called a kingdom—if only it was ruled by a personage of royal blood instead of a low-life pirate chieftain with a price on his head. On the island of Madagascar, for example, many individual pirates live in houses surrounded by a stockade.

* A pirate compound in Madagascar

The Isle of Tortuga

In the 1630s Tortuga became a haven for buccaneers, who launched raids against Spanish cities in Central America.

Notable Dangers

The alleys of a pirate port teem with riffraff at all hours. Decent folk cannot walk the streets even in daylight without fear of being affronted by thieves, murderers, kidnappers, hucksters and every other kind of vagabond.

OFF-WATCH ACTIVITY Familiarise yourself with piratical haunts so that you are better able to track down the rogues. Invent a suitable name and design a sign for a pirate tavern.

Lesson 19:
The Galley

That noxious pirate Arabella Drummond's BOLD ADVENTURE is a modern sort of galley, and to be feared as she moves swiftly both under sail and when propelled by the oars. If we encounter her on a windless day we may find that we run into difficulties. Indeed, there is a story that this very thing occurred when Drummond met and captured a French merchant ship named LA BELLE DAME DE GUIANA.

* Arabella Drummond

BOLD ADVENTURE

* The design of the BOLD ADVENTURE was copied from that of the ADVENTURE, the galley given to the infamous Captain Kidd when he was appointed an official pirate hunter.

* The BOLD ADVENTURE'S oars, thirteen to a side, are located below the gun deck. The openings for the oars can be closed with watertight doors when the sea is rough.

Manning the Oars

You have already learned how the Barbary pirates make slaves of their captives and put them to ceaseless labour rowing their galleys. But there is more to good rowing than just muscle power. Timing is important and so is the spirit of the rowers. No matter how hard slaves are whipped, they will never match the enthusiasm of honest seamen with a legitimate aim.

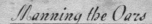

BARBARY GALLEY

A Barbary galley, which sits low in the water, is easily recognised by its large number of oars and its distinctive triangular sails.

WARSHIP

* How the BOLD ADVENTURE outmanoeuvred LA BELLE DAME.

1. There is no wind, so both ships are becalmed.

BOLD ADVENTURE

BELLE DAME

3. The BOLD ADVENTURE shoots away LA BELLE DAME'S rudder. LA BELLE DAME surrenders and the BOLD ADVENTURE draws alongside.

2. The BOLD ADVENTURE uses her oars to approach LA BELLE DAME.

By using oar power to manoeuvre behind LA BELLE DAME, Drummond was able to fire a broadside that disabled the merchant ship.

A warship may carry 48 or more cannon, but the size and weight of the vessel mean that it is not as fast as a galley when under sail.

OFF-WATCH ACTIVITY In these pirate-hunting lessons we are concentrating on pirate ships. However, we ought to be proud of the warships that keep our coasts free from pirates. See what you can find out about some of history's most famous warships.

Lesson 20:
Pirate Weapons

Pirate ships may bristle with cannon of every size, but these are largely for bluster rather than bombardment. No sailor likes to see a ship lost to the ocean depths, and pirates have even more reason to keep their prizes afloat. They want to capture their victim and its cargo intact, so that it will be of the greatest benefit to them—no pirate profits if his prize lies at the bottom of the ocean.

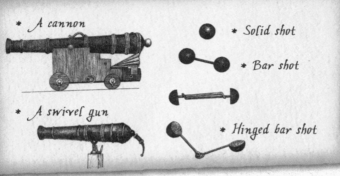

* A cannon

* Solid shot

* Bar shot

* A swivel gun

* Hinged bar shot

* Grapeshot does not damage a ship very much, but the small balls are deadly to anyone in the firing line.

The main guns are mounted on wheeled platforms so their recoil does not shake the ship's timbers apart. Swivel guns are located fore and aft so they can fire over the bow or stern. A solid shot can punch a hole through both sides of a ship. To avoid damaging a prize, pirate gunners often use bar shot, with two projectiles joined together, to bring down masts and rigging.

* Musket

* Sword

* Powder horn

* Dagger

* Boarding axe

* Pistols

Muskets and pistols are stored loaded and ready for use, while knives, swords and boarding axes are kept razor sharp.

Firing a Broadside

If all the guns on one side of a ship are used at once this is called a broadside. Pirate gunners must take special care about their aim — if they aim too low they will hit the target below the water line and it may sink.

Once at close quarters, pirates swarm aboard their unfortunate prey using boat hooks and grappling irons.

Master the Maze

Finish

Start

OFF-WATCH ACTIVITY A bo'sun must be a skilled navigator to keep the ship out of trouble. Can you complete the maze above and sail your ship safely through pirate-infested waters to recover the treasure, skirting around both cannon fire from forts and ships, and dangerous rocky islands?

Lesson 21:
The Cautionary Tale of Jack Rackham

Bo'suns no doubt realise that although many pirates may appear gallant, they are often cowardly drunkards at heart. Such is the case of Jack Rackham, who was captured hiding below decks, too drunk to fight, leaving Anne Bonny and Mary Read to defend his ship.

Before Rackham became a captain, he served as quartermaster aboard a brigantine commanded by a certain Captain Vane. The quartermaster was responsible for keeping the ship well supplied and issuing rations and ammunition. Rackham seems to have been popular with the ship's crew, because when they turned against Vane for refusing to attack a French warship, they elected Rackham as their new captain.

Vane's ship had been based on the island of New Providence in the Bahamas and, just like the unfortunate Edward England, he had fled when the new governor arrived in 1717. Instead of crossing the ocean like England, however, Vane had chosen to sail southwards into the Caribbean Sea. The new captain saw no reason to quarrel with this decision, and so he joined the ranks of the Caribbean pirates.

Rackham attacked merchant ships sailing between Jamaica and Bermuda, and soon acquired a reputation for ferocity along with his infamous nickname. He is thought to have acquired this name—Calico Jack—from his custom of wearing bright clothes made of printed Indian cloth, called calico.

Members of his piratical crew were every bit as colourful as their captain—especially the two women, Anne Bonny and Mary Read. Bonny left her husband to join Rackham's crew, sailing with him when he fled New Providence. On board she wore men's clothing and fought fiercely alongside the others, earning her great respect among the crew.

* Rackham's appearance was as colourful as his reputation.

Mary Read was a runaway who disguised herself as a boy in order to find work. So disguised, she had served in both the army and navy before joining Rackham's pirate crew. She was a dead shot with a pistol and very handy with a cutlass—she once killed another pirate in a seashore duel. Her disguise as a man was reported to be so convincing that Anne Bonny is said to have fallen in love with 'him'!

On one occasion Rackham's vessel was spied by a Spanish warship off Cuba. The Spaniards were in a sprightly mood because they had just captured an English sloop. Knowing that he could not win any kind of battle against a fully-armed warship, Rackham decided to use cunning instead. Waiting until darkness fell, he and his companions, including Mary Read, took to the jolly boat and rowed silently out to the captured sloop. They quickly overpowered the Spanish guards and sailed silently away while the Spaniards' attention was focused on their old ship. The next morning, the Spanish were infuriated to find that their sloop had been 'replaced' by Rackham's leaky old tub!

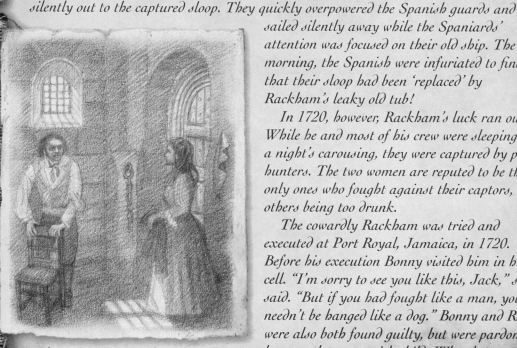

✻ Bonny and Read fighting side by side

In 1720, however, Rackham's luck ran out. While he and most of his crew were sleeping off a night's carousing, they were captured by pirate hunters. The two women are reputed to be the only ones who fought against their captors, the others being too drunk.

The cowardly Rackham was tried and executed at Port Royal, Jamaica, in 1720. Before his execution Bonny visited him in his cell. "I'm sorry to see you like this, Jack," she said. "But if you had fought like a man, you needn't be hanged like a dog." Bonny and Read were also both found guilty, but were pardoned because they were with child. What became of them, and their piratical offspring, is unknown.

✻ Anne Bonny says a final farewell to Rackham in his condemned cell.

Roster of Captain's Duties

* Bring piratical rogues to justice
* Take captured spoils to port to be valued
* Pay the crew their share and deliver the balance to the ship's owners
* Ensure the ship is kept in seaworthy condition
* Promote members of the crew as you see fit
* Sit in judgement over disputes among the crew
* Investigate reports of buried pirate treasure
* Decipher secret codes used by pirates
* Plot a course between any two ports in the world
* Show bravery and leadership in battle
* If all is lost, you shall go down with your ship, having saved as many hands as fortune allows... and may God have mercy on your soul.

Hours of Work

As captain it is your duty to attend to the ship whenever there is call for your superior skills and knowledge of the sea. You must ensure that you get sufficient rest to enable you always to be alert when on duty. Therefore, you may set your hours of work and rest so as to best suit your circumstances.

* As captain of an official pirate-hunting ship, you are expected to maintain a smart and sober appearance at all times. You will most certainly not adopt any of the outlandish fashions that are affected by many pirate captains, such as the wearing of flamboyant jewellery or the carrying of parrots. You must consider yourself an emissary for your country, behaving at all times in a courageous and dignified fashion.

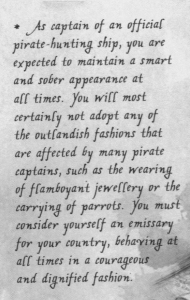

The Rank of
CAPTAIN

You are hereby raised to the rank of captain—a promotion that will in due course be confirmed in writing by my superiors in Boston. Please accept my very warm and personal congratulations. It is my great pleasure to present you with your first commission: I am making you captain of the SWIFTBUCK, lately recovered from that same villainous Captain Carlton whom I had fortune enough to capture and who now languishes in chains in Boston awaiting execution.

If you will accept some advice from one with no small amount of experience in these matters—treat your crew fairly at all times, but do not allow them too much liberty, and always be steadfast and confident in your respect for the letter of the law.

Now, Captain, I wish you Godspeed and good luck with your new command. Together, we shall make all piratical rogues rue the day they dared put to sea with evil intentions festering in their black hearts.

William

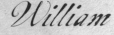

Lesson 22:
Chinese Pirates

Your new duties as captain of a pirate-hunting ship empower you to seek out, capture or destroy pirates, not merely in local waters but in all parts of the world. If you intend to voyage to the Far East, you would be well advised to learn all you can about the pirates there before you set out. The coastline around the port of Canton in China is a notorious haunt of particularly savage pirates. These rogues attack in such large numbers that none but the bravest and boldest sea captains may hope to withstand their onslaught.

* Do not be deceived by the dazzling variety of silken clothes worn by Chinese pirates. Beneath their coloured finery these are deadly fighters. They practise swordplay constantly, some favouring two short swords, others choosing a single, longer blade.

Oriental Weapons

The finest oriental blades are rumoured to come from the islands of Japan, where foreigners are forbidden. Chinese swords, however, should not in any way be considered inferior. This sword, to be wielded with two hands, is sharp enough to slice through armour with a single blow.

* A two-handed Chinese blade

CHINESE JUNK

Chinese Junks

The most commonly sighted ship on the China Sea is the junk. The word is not a comment upon the ship's worth, as this local craft is most seaworthy. Each of the masts carries a single square sail made of cloth or woven strips of bamboo.

* Each pirate has his own junk that is both the family home and their means of income.

OFF-WATCH ACTIVITY Increase your knowledge of Chinese pirates and their ways by discovering all you can about the pirate Zheng Zhilong.

Lesson 23:
Grace O'Malley

As you have already learned, some women have been known to turn pirate—a choice of career that is most unladylike and greatly to be deplored. One of the most infamous of these seafaring harpies was Grace O'Malley—her villainous exploits against English ships made her something of a heroine in her native Ireland.

Grace O'Malley was born in about 1530, the daughter of a local chieftain on the west coast of Ireland. The family business was a mixture of farming, trading, raiding their neighbours, fighting against the English and piracy. When she was young Grace cut her hair in order to make her father take her to sea, earning herself the nickname Gráinne Mhaol, or Granuaile ('mhaol' means 'short-haired' in Gaelic).

Her first husband was killed in a revenge attack, so O'Malley moved back to her father's house and took command of the family fleet, where she soon proved herself to be a skilful and fearless captain. In 1566 she married a chieftain named Burke and took up residence in Rockfleet Castle, overlooking the windswept Atlantic Ocean.

Among her fleet of some 20 ships were a number of galleys, which, being oar powered, were able to manoeuvre when close to the windward shores of western Ireland. Chief among her targets were the fat merchant ships of the English overlords. O'Malley infuriated the English so much that, in 1574, they sent an expedition against her to lay siege to Rockfleet Castle. O'Malley managed to repulse this attack, but three years later she was captured while out raiding and was imprisoned in Limerick Gaol for some 18 months.

* For some unfathomable reason a strange form of mutual respect developed between the noble and virtuous Elizabeth, Queen of England, and the villainous O'Malley, 'Queen of Pirates'.

Soon after her release, her husband died and O'Malley found herself in a greatly weakened position. A new English governor sent a much larger force and her fleet of ships was seized and confiscated.

After these events, the impudent harpy took it upon herself to write a most remarkable letter to Her Majesty Queen Elizabeth herself, claiming to be a loyal subject who was merely defending her territory against hostile and aggressive neighbours. While the Queen was still pondering her reply, O'Malley's son Tibbot was arrested and charged with rebellion, which carried the same penalty as piracy—death. O'Malley immediately boarded a ship and sailed across the Irish Sea in order to make a personal appeal to the Queen. History has recorded neither the details of her voyage nor what was said between the two women. All that is known is that they met at Greenwich in September 1593. A few days later, Queen Elizabeth wrote to the governor and ordered him to release Tibbot and pay O'Malley a regular allowance. These instructions were obeyed, but her ships fortunately remained under lock and key.

Not until another governor was appointed in 1597 was O'Malley, now aged about 70, allowed to put to sea once more. She died in 1603, the same year as Elizabeth, and remained stubborn and intemperate to the end.

Lesson 24:
Pirate Treasure

When men speak of treasure they mean gold, silver and jewels, and there is no pirate that does not love these things above all else. Gold, of unparalleled value to pirates, is as much desired by kings as by those seafaring rascals. Silver, although of lesser value, is the basis for the coinage that ordinary men and women use every day, and the attraction of precious jewels is glitteringly obvious.

Withstanding Temptation

As a pirate hunter, you should be on constant guard against temptation, not only in yourself but also throughout your crew. When stolen treasure is recovered, you must ensure than none of it sticks to the fingers of your men.

All That Glitters

Although small nuggets of gold may be found by sifting through gravel in certain rivers, underground deposits, such as those in Mexico, are the most reliable source. Farther south, at a place called Potosí, the Spanish have discovered a mountain made almost entirely of silver-bearing rock.

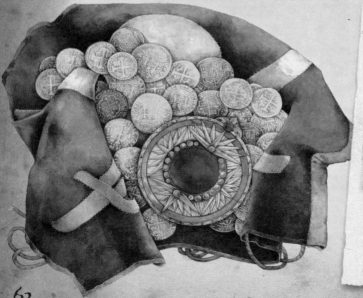

* When that scurvy privateer turned pirate Captain Kidd was arrested, the authorities recovered treasure worth more than 10,000 pounds.

* The Spanish often turn metal into coinage before it is shipped to Europe.

Silver coins with a value of eight Spanish reales are known as pieces of eight.

Spanish conquistadors looted huge amounts of gold from the temples, tombs and treasuries of the Inca people in Peru. Many hundreds of masks and statues of exquisite workmanship were melted down to make coins.

* Cannon

* Bales of tobacco

* Barrel of salt fish

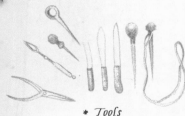

* Tools

* Wood

* Cloth

The reality of pirate life is that a good haul is anything that can be sold. Food, cannon and gunpowder are especially welcome as they can always be put to good use. Sometimes a pirate captain must even be able to act the part of a cloth merchant or a tobacco salesman.

OFF-WATCH ACTIVITY A useful method of familiarising yourself with different coins is to take coin rubbings. Place tracing paper over a coin you wish to rub, then shade over the top using a soft pencil, making an impression of the coin for future reference.

Lesson 25:
Treasure Maps & Secret Codes

Buried treasure is a very scarce commodity—most pirates are spendthrifts and gamblers who let money dribble through their fingers like water. Pirates are more likely to be treasure hunters than buriers, but there are some exceptions. Both the villainous Captain Kidd and the virtuous Sir Francis Drake are believed to have hidden at least one treasure chest on Oak Island, near Nova Scotia.

Map of Goat Island

N

Sharpe's Bay

Windy Bay

X

Mountainous and inhospitable

Wool Strand

Fall's Anchoring

Goat Quarters

Sugarloaf Key

Water Hole

Reef Point

Great Rock

S

Rocky Point

Goat Hills

Great Key

There is another supposed 'treasure island' in the Pacific near the coast of Chile. Nobody knows for sure whether there is any treasure buried here, but at least one castaway, Alexander Selkirk—the real-life Robinson Crusoe—was marooned here. From scribblings in the journal of the rogue Captain Carton, it appears that he may have hidden some ill-gotten booty on this remote island himself.

Hidden treasure!

Some say that Blackbeard buried a loot that has never been found. I have had the fortune to come across this map and a coded message—could they be clues to the whereabouts of Blackbeard's treasure?

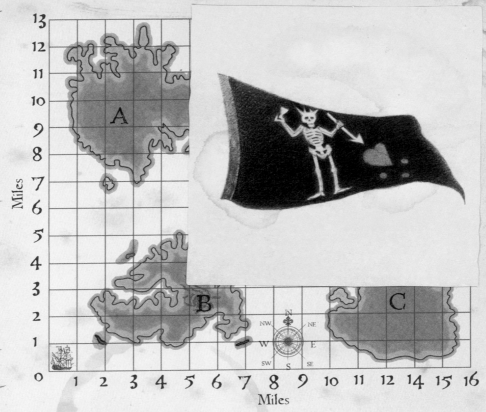

OFF-WATCH ACTIVITY You must get to know your enemy. Imagine you have some treasure to hide. Plan where you would hide it on one of the islands above, then leave instructions about the location of your treasure in code.

Lesson 26:
Pirate Punishments

As captain, you are responsible for maintaining discipline, making judgements and ordering punishments. On law-abiding ships it is normally the bo'sun who carries out the punishments, so you will not be expected to get your own hands dirty. On pirate ships, however, it is the captain himself who is most likely to punish offenders, and in ways more savage than aboard a lawful ship.

Pirates have a range of grisly punishments for captives who refuse to give up their goods, or for other pirates who disobey the pirates' code. These punishments must be voted on by the crew before being carried out.

✸ A pirate may be marooned on a desert island with only one shot in his pistol and a single bottle of water.

✸ A pirate or enemy captive may be hanged from the yardarm as a warning to others.

✸ Pirates make their victims dance around the mainmast by pricking their legs with cutlasses.

✸ If a pirate has not committed a serious crime he may be flogged with the cat-o'-nine-tails, but this punishment is more common aboard naval vessels.

✸ Occasionally a pirate may be keelhauled. This involves tying the pirate's hands to a rope and dragging him underneath the ship. If he is lucky, he will avoid the sharp barnacles and lurking sharks and live to tell the tale.

✸ If pirates want to get rid of their victims quickly, they may simply throw them overboard, where the hapless sailors will have a long swim if they do not want to drown.

Rough Justice

Pirate punishments are swift and harsh as these rogues have no regard for lawful authority. The fact that they are engaged in piracy means they face the death penalty if captured. In consequence, they have little respect for human life and the sufferings of their victims are often considered entertainment for the rest of the crew.

✷ The dreaded cat-o-nine-tails

Fact or Fancy?

There is a fanciful notion
that pirates are accustomed to
making their victims walk to
their doom along a plank
placed over the side of a vessel.
However, although many
admit to having heard of this
punishment, I have yet to
encounter a pirate or a pirate
hunter who has actually
witnessed anyone engaging
in this practice.

Marooning

Marooning is the punishment pirates fear the most — more so than being hanged at the
gallows. Although setting a man on an empty island instead of throwing him overboard
seems a kindly thing to do, it is actually a wicked torture. Alone upon an island with but
faint hope of rescue, the victim must decide whether to go slowly mad from loneliness or
end it quickly with the pistol his former shipmates have so thoughtfully provided.

OFF-WATCH ACTIVITY Imagine you have been marooned on a desert island. Write
your own sea shanty to sing to pass the time until you are rescued. It ought to rhyme
if possible. Start with the line, 'A sailor's life is a life on the sea'.

Lesson 27:
The Carrack & Galleon

It is possible that your voyaging will lead you to encounter examples of some older types of craft, as many of these floating antiques are still seaworthy. The two vessels you are most likely to meet are the galleon, which may give a good account of itself in battle; and the carrack, which is a lumbering beast of a merchant ship, nowadays used for cheap, bulk cargo if used at all.

Sir Francis Drake

Drake, who died in 1596, was an English soldier, seafarer, explorer and privateer. He attacked Spanish ports in the Caribbean and helped defeat the Spanish Armada in 1588. Aboard his galleon the PELICAN, Drake circumnavigated the globe.

The Galleon

A galleon is a sixteenth-century sailing ship that, with its extended prow, looks somewhat similar to the oar-powered galley. Galleons were much favoured by the Spanish, who used these armed ships to carry cargos of riches from the Americas to Europe.

* Even large galleons are vulnerable when pirates attack from several directions at once. The captain of the ship cannot concentrate his cannon on any one of the attackers' vessels without allowing the others to get close enough for their bloodthirsty occupants to clamber aboard.

The largest galleons were built by the Spaniards to carry gold and silver across the Atlantic. Sometimes an entire year's production would be crammed aboard a single vessel. When Drake captured the galleon CACAFUEGO it took his crew six days to transfer all the treasure to the hold of the PELICAN.

CARRACK

Francis Drake chanced upon the treasure galleon known as CACAFUEGO off the coast of Panama. Through skilful use of cannon fire, the privateer first disabled his Spanish prize by shooting away the masts and rudder, so that it could be boarded and captured.

OFF-WATCH ACTIVITY Now you are familiar with the ships of pirates and pirate hunters, draw a design for your own perfect pirate-hunting ship. Who knows—perhaps one day you will be able to commission your ship to be built.

Lesson 28:
The Cautionary Tale of Henry Morgan

Our final tale is the story of a Welsh privateer who was tempted into dishonesty but who, in later life, saw the error of his lawless ways and became a pirate hunter. Henry Morgan was perhaps the greatest of the privateer captains who waged unofficial war against the Spanish in the Caribbean and Central America. No Spanish ship or town was safe from his attack, and he is said to have carried away treasure worth millions of dollars.

* Morgan gained most of his success fighting on dry land rather than at sea.

As a young man Henry Morgan was sent to the Caribbean in 1655 as part of an English expedition against the Spanish. The expedition failed to shift the Spanish from the island of Hispaniola, so the English settled in Jamaica instead.

In about 1660 Morgan, who was by then a ship's captain, obtained letters of marque allowing him to attack Spanish ships. Although he managed to take several galleons, Morgan was dissatisfied with his rewards, especially because he had to share the spoils with the authorities. He decided to try his luck at dry-land piracy and began plundering the Spanish towns along the mainland coast. His main tactic was to attack in overwhelming numbers—he often had more than 1,000 vicious buccaneers under his command—and he was usually successful.

In 1668 the English encouraged Morgan to attack the Spanish in Cuba. He easily captured the city of Puerto Principe and then marched his men through dense jungle to subdue the three forts

* Many of Morgan's men were recruited from that den of iniquity called Tortuga.

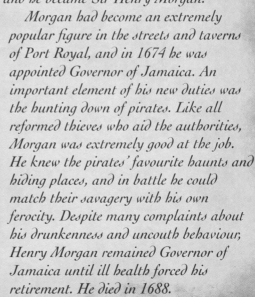

that guarded the larger and richer city of Portobelo. He spent three weeks looting every building in that city and crushed a Spanish counterattack. His buccaneers returned to Jamaica with their ships heavily laden with stolen silver and gold.

In 1671, however, a daring raid on the city of Panama provided the buccaneers with meagre pickings and they fell out among themselves. The Spanish made furious complaints to the English king, Charles II, about Morgan's attacks, and Morgan was eventually arrested and taken to London. But instead of doling out a punishment, King Charles rewarded Morgan with a knighthood, and he became Sir Henry Morgan.

Morgan had become an extremely popular figure in the streets and taverns of Port Royal, and in 1674 he was appointed Governor of Jamaica. An important element of his new duties was the hunting down of pirates. Like all reformed thieves who aid the authorities, Morgan was extremely good at the job. He knew the pirates' favourite haunts and hiding places, and in battle he could match their savagery with his own ferocity. Despite many complaints about his drunkenness and uncouth behaviour, Henry Morgan remained Governor of Jamaica until ill health forced his retirement. He died in 1688.

* Morgan's ruthless buccaneers stripped Portobelo of all its valuables.

Appendix 1:
A History of Piracy

c.1200 B.C.   Widespread disruption of Mediterranean trade is caused by marauding 'Sea Peoples'.

c.700 B.C.   Etruscan pirates raid Greek cities in southern Italy.

c. 530 B.C.   The tyrant Polycrates rules the island of Samos where more than 100 pirate ships are based.

* Greek ships in port

78 B.C.   The Roman politician Julius Caesar is captured by pirates and held for ransom.

67 B.C.   The Roman general Pompey the Great leads a fleet of 500 ships against the pirates of southern Turkey.

c.360   The Romans build forts along the shores of Britain for defence against pirates.

* A Viking longboat

c.850   Vikings make piratical raids from their newly established base at Dublin.

1470s   The Barbarossa brothers are born in the Mediterranean.

* The Barbarossa brothers

| 1492 | Christopher Columbus discovers America, landing on San Salvador. |

1504   The elder Barbarossa brother captures two galleys belonging to the Pope.

1523   The French privateer Jean Fleury captures a Spanish galleon full of Aztec gold.

1553   Francois 'Peg Leg' Le Clerc ravages the island of Puerto Rico.

1555   French pirates capture Havana, Cuba.

1566   Grace O'Malley takes up residence at Rockfleet Castle, from where she launches attacks against ships along Ireland's Atlantic coast.

1566   Dutch privateers and pirates join forces against the Spanish and become known as the 'Sea Beggars'.

1570   The French pirate Jacques de Sores massacres 39 Spanish priests at Las Palmas.

1571   Many corsair ships are among the Turkish fleet defeated by the Venetians and Spanish at the battle of Lepanto in the Mediterranean.

1574   The Sea Beggars annihilate the Spanish fleet in the North Sea and drive the Spanish out of Holland.

1579	The privateer Francis Drake captures the Spanish galleon CACAFUEGO off the coast of Panama.
1620s	The first buccaneers settle on the island of Tortuga and begin to attack Spanish ships.
1653	The captain 'El Pirata' disguises his men as friars so they can gain entrance to, and ransack, the city of Santiago in Cuba.

* Sir Francis Drake

1665	The buccaneers of Tortuga pledge allegiance to the King of France.
1667	The pirate captain l'Ollonais pillages the port of Maracaibo in Venezuela.
1668	A joint expedition between Henry Morgan and French buccaneers is abandoned after one of their ships explodes, killing more than 200 men.

* l'Ollonais

1668	L'Ollonais is shipwrecked on a remote Caribbean island and eaten by cannibals.
1671	Henry Morgan loots the city of Panama.
1682	The buccaneer Michel de Grammont's army captures the port of Veracruz from the Spanish.
1694	Henry Every begins his piratical career.

1695	The pirate Thomas Tew is decapitated during a sword fight with an Indian pirate.

1701	Captain William Kidd is executed and his body hung in chains.

1717	Governor Woodes Rogers arrives in the Bahamas with the intention of driving pirates from their haunts on the island of New Providence.

* William Kidd, hanging in chains

1718	Edward 'Blackbeard' Teach holds the biggest ever pirate reunion at his home on an island off the coast of North Carolina.

1718	Major Stede Bonnet is executed for piracy at Charles Town.

1720	Jack Rackham, Anne Bonny and Mary Read are captured. Rackham is executed in Jamaica.

* Bartholomew Roberts's flag

1722	The Welsh pirate Bartholomew Roberts is killed in a battle off the coast of West Africa.

1724	Captain Johnson publishes his book 'A General History of the Robberies and Murders of the Most Notorious Pyrates'.

Appendix 2:
A Glossary of Nautical Terms

AFT	In the direction of the rear of a ship; towards the stern.
ANCHOR	A heavy object attached to a rope and dropped overboard to secure a ship to the sea bed.
BACKSTAFF	An early navigational device used to determine the sun's position.
BO'SUN	The shortened form of boatswain; a person in charge of a boat, or the second-in-command of a ship.
BOW	The front end of a ship (the pointed end!).
BUCCANEER	A European settler in the Caribbean who turned to piracy.
CAPSTAN	A man-powered windlass (winding machine) used for hauling up the anchor.
CAREEN	To scrape off weeds or barnacles from a ship's hull beneath the water line (the ship must be hauled out of the water first).
CROW'S NEST	A lookout platform located near the top of the tallest mast.
DIVIDERS	Two rods hinged at one end, used to measure distances on a chart.
FORE	In the direction of the front of a ship; towards the bow.
FREEBOOTER	Another name for a buccaneer, especially one who is of Dutch origin.
GALLEY	A type of ship that can be powered by oars as well as by sails.
GRAPESHOT	Small lead balls that are loaded into a cannon.

p. 53

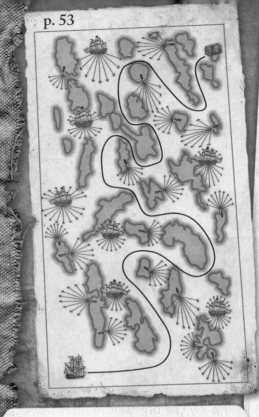

SOLUTIONS

p. 3 On cracking the rest of code on page 3 and deciphering the message, it is evident to the publisher that Captain Lubber's hope that the map would reveal the whereabouts of a missing treasure was not to be fulfilled. It is possible that the coded message was written either to throw bounty hunters off the scent of a real treasure, or simply as an idle prank.

A = B	H = I	O = P	V = W
B = C	I = J	P = Q	W = X
C = D	J = K	Q = R	X = Y
D = E	K = L	R = S	Y = Z
E = F	L = M	S = T	Z = A
F = G	M = N	T = U	
G = H	N = O	U = V	

TRANSLATION OF CODED MESSAGE:
IF YOU SEEK TREASURE IN THIS PLACE, YOU ARE ON A WILD GOOSE CHASE.

p. 13 The captain will receive $1,500. Each able seaman will receive $100.

p.65

TRANSLATION OF CODED MESSAGE:
Sea hazards keep the enemy away,
Only the bravest will find a way.
Follow my route through the treacherous sea,
To find my treasure on island D.

Five miles north, three east, two northeast, one east, two southeast, six east, five north, two west

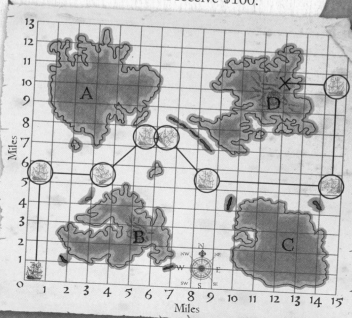

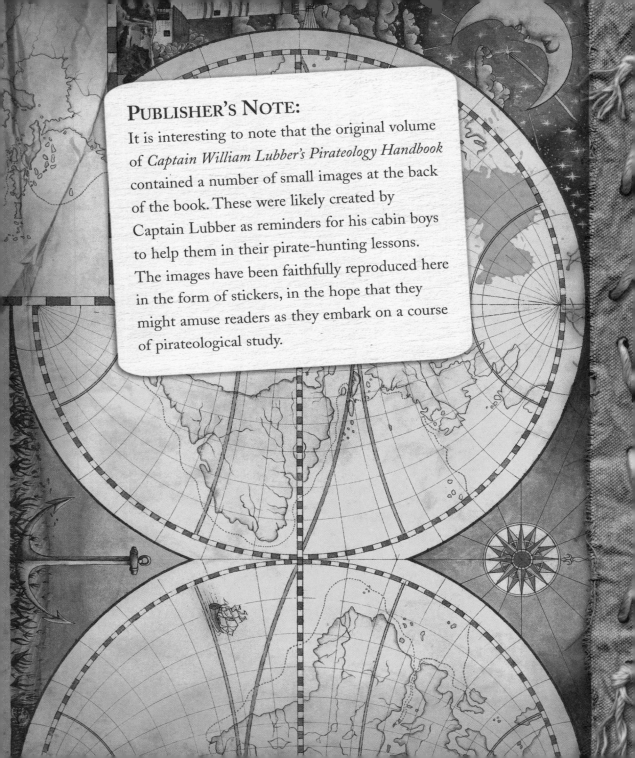

PUBLISHER'S NOTE:

It is interesting to note that the original volume of *Captain William Lubber's Pirateology Handbook* contained a number of small images at the back of the book. These were likely created by Captain Lubber as reminders for his cabin boys to help them in their pirate-hunting lessons. The images have been faithfully reproduced here in the form of stickers, in the hope that they might amuse readers as they embark on a course of pirateological study.